For my children: Lindsay, David, and Evan.

Thank you to:

Mark, for loving nature with me;

Alice Janke, my faithful friend, for helping me to take the leap and write;

Marian Nelson and Kris Yankee, for seeing the message in my story and delivering it to children;

and Rita Viscount, for bringing this story to life with graceful beauty.

"I'm going to be the first to see the waterfall!" shouted David.

"No! I get to be first this time!" yelled Evan. The two boys pushed each other and scrambled up the path.

Mimi the Inchworm
let out a heavy sigh
after the boys ran past her.
"Why do you sound so dreary?"
asked a dragonfly.
"Every time kids race past me," Mimi
began, "I can't stop thinking how small and
unimportant I am."

"I believe that everything on this Earth is important. All living things have a purpose," the dragonfly explained. "I've never heard that before. What do you mean?" asked Mimi.

"All I can do is inch along on my wooden post or scoot across the top of this fence, while everyone else goes running past me to see the powerful waterfall. I wish I were fast and big and powerful too!" cried Mimi. "I'm only an inch long."

The smiling dragonfly was silent for a moment. Suddenly, he lifted from his leaf and glided softly, landing next to Mimi. "I know for a fact that you are important," he said boldly. "You will see—if you pay close attention."

Mimi slumped and began to turn back toward her post. "It's useless," she said. "I really can't do anything special except stretch and scrunch myself into a horseshoe. I'm so small, no one ever notices me."

"Well, I've just noticed you now, haven't I?" questioned the dragonfly.
"Oh, I didn't mean to be rude—" Mimi started.

"I think I know," interrupted the dragonfly. "You need to feel deep in your heart that you make a difference in this world, right?" Mimi scrunched. "I'm just so small," she said.

They were interrupted by one of the boys Mimi had just seen. He flopped his elbows on top of the wooden fence, causing the dragonfly to lift quickly away.

"Of course he always has to beat me in a race," Evan moaned to himself. "Of course David gets to the waterfall first because he's older and faster than me. I wish I weren't so small and slow."

Evan sighed heavily and closed his eyes. While his eyes were still closed, Mimi inched toward him. When she was near his elbow, he opened his eyes.

"An inchworm!" Evan gasped excitedly. He bent down close and became very still. Mimi could tell he still needed a smile, so she scrunched for him and made the most perfect horseshoe.

Then she reached up high and stretched herself out, swaying side to side before landing on his forearm. Evan squinted and giggled.

Mimi started to feel giggly too. She tickled her way from his arm to his wrist as she inched down toward his small hand.

"Hey!" Evan called to his family. "Come see what I found!"

"What is it?" David asked.
"It's an inchworm, and it's so cool.
You have to see this!"

"Whoa!" David exclaimed when he saw Mimi on the young boy's arm. Mimi stretched extra long and scrunched before their eyes. When Evan's face was close to her, she stretched out and touched the tip of his nose.

The two boys erupted in laughter and watched in amazement
until their parents called them to go home.

Evan placed Mimi back on her wooden post and took
a long moment to look at her.
"I won't forget you," he whispered.

"Isn't that the coolest little thing ever?" Evan asked.

"Yeah," David replied. "I wish I had found that. You're lucky because you always find the tiniest and most interesting things in nature."

TAKE ONLY PICTURES
LEAVE ONLY FOOTPRINTS

The boys looked closely at Mimi one last time, and then
they turned and walked down the path with their parents.

"That was so amazing! We should come back here again!" Mimi heard them say.

"Did you see that?" Mimi asked the dragonfly.
"I sure did," he said, nodding to her. "The smiles on those boys' faces were put there by you!"

"That felt incredible!" Mimi said. "I never realized that all I have to do is just be myself, and I can make a difference to someone else. If I hadn't been right here, that boy would have left this beautiful place without a smile on his face and happiness in his heart."

"You are absolutely right," the dragonfly agreed. "You are very important in this world."

When the sun dipped below the horizon, Mimi knew in her heart that, as tiny as she was, the world was a better place with her in it.

Visiting Tahquamenon Falls State Park

If you were to cross the Mackinac Bridge and head north to Paradise, Michigan, you might actually find an inchworm like Mimi in Tahquamenon Falls State Park. Before you found one though, you would most likely stop to read signs that would tell you amazing facts about the wilderness around you—facts about its vast forty-five thousand acres of beautiful land and more than forty miles of hiking trails. Of course, you might also learn that the Upper Falls is nearly two hundred feet wide and drops about fifty feet to the river below! You could also find out about the thirteen different lakes or the one hundred and twenty-five different species of birds that nest there. You could see something as magnificent as a waterfall, as large as a moose, or as tiny as an inchworm. All you have to do is pay close attention.

How to Watch an Inchworm

It takes practice to be quiet and still enough to see the tiniest things in nature. If you come upon an inchworm, wait for it to come near you rather than trying to pick it up. You wouldn't want to squish it accidentally, because then it couldn't become the beautiful moth it is destined to be. If you want it to visit with you for a while, just put out your finger when it's in its horseshoe shape and perhaps it will climb aboard. Of course, it may just be busy eating leaves. Did you know that inchworms feed on the leaves of trees and shrubs all spring until they burrow underground to make a cocoon and wait to become a moth? They are actually different sizes, starting at about one centimeter long. Their name comes from the way that they scrunch and scoot their bodies to "inch" forward.

How to See a Smiling Dragonfly

You can usually find a dragonfly flying from leaf to leaf. They don't eat leaves; they just use them as landing and launching pads. They don't breathe fire like dragons in fairy tales either. They breathe through their tail and eat mosquitoes with their mouth. They actually look like they are smiling because of the shape of their jaw. To see a dragonfly's smile, hold out your hand and let it land on your finger. Then slowly bring it close to you and look up into its face. You may have to try several times if it keeps flying away. You could also try to get one to land on a small mirror and look down at the mirror to see its smile. It might like to see its own smile too!

About the Author

Sue Beth Balash began writing as a teenager. As a young girl, she spent time reading, writing poems, and painting outside among nature. She is a wife, mother, and elementary school teacher. If you ask her, she will tell you that one of her favorite things to do is to read stories to children. She read to her own children every night in their growing years and still reads to her teenage sons once in a while. She and her family live in Commerce Township, Michigan. Together, they enjoy camping, hiking, golfing, beachcombing, birdwatching, and sightseeing around Michigan and nearby national parks.

About the Illustrator

Rita Viscount was a master doodler in school, where a notebook was not safe. As a child, her father allowed Rita to splash and paint murals on the walls in her bedroom. Rita's two youngest children, Dan and Tamara, as well as her grandchildren, Isaac and Tala, have all gladly acted as her models. She and her family enjoy camping and exploring the great outdoors, as she believes that one never knows where the next adventure may be. Mainly a self taught painter, Rita is a member of Sarnia Artists' Workshop in Canada, as well as a member of "The 6 + 1 Art Group". You can view her work at www.atirstudio.com.

JUVENILE FICTION / Social Issues / Self-Esteem & Self-Reliance

Can an inchworm really make a difference in the world? That's the question that bothers Mimi, an inchworm, as she watches the world around her in Tahquamenon Falls State Park in Michigan. But when a little boy is upset about a race with his brother, Mimi realizes that her small stature can leave a big impact on those around her.

"Each page of *Mimi the Inchworm* is a delight. Savor them, like warm, sunny days by the Tahquamenon Falls in Michigan's Upper Peninsula. This book warms the soul."
~Bob Sornson, Ph.D., founder of the Early Learning Foundation

"Set at northern Michigan's breathtaking Tahquamenon Falls, *Mimi the Inchworm* reminds readers that everyone is important, special, and unique no matter how small. Informative Author's Notes link the story to an appreciation of nature. This heartwarming book, with its inspiring text and beautiful illustrations, will be loved by all."
~ Rebecca Blaharski, School Library Media Specialist

$10.95 US

ISBN 978-1-933916-44-6

51095>

9 781933 916446

FERNE PRESS